My warning, you must heed,
Before we begin.
For a terrible tale,
Lies just within.

Our story begins with Bunker the Pug.

He was neither large nor tall
In fact, he was rather quite small

And yet you might query,
"Was he brave?"

...No.
Not at all.

His troubles began when the work week did start.

For Bunker loved his dear daddy
With all of his heart.

"MMMMMM," whined Bunker
As his daddy did depart.

Boogers oozed from his nose,
And he eked out a fart.

As he pulled from the driveway,
Bunker moped to the den.
To await his daddy's return,
Bunks would nap until then.

T'was here the horror began to unfold
A terror of which could not be foretold.

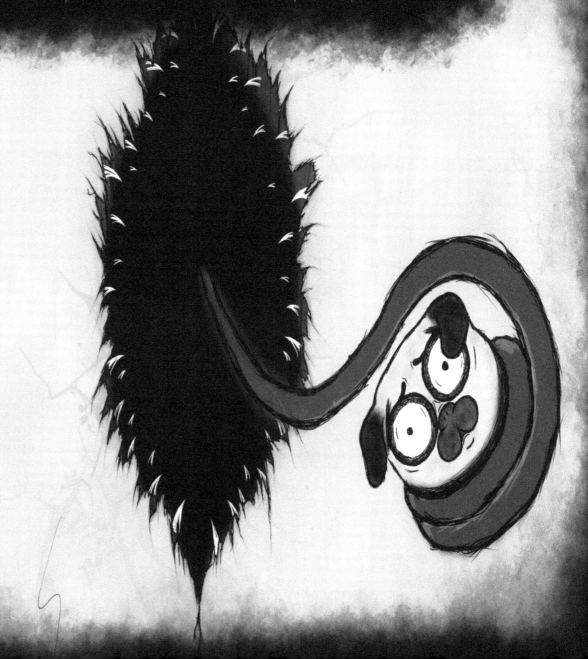

Down into the cushions,
Our dear Bunker did drop.
Where the darkness was darkest
Even the rhyme scheme did stop

Like a sack of potatoes,
Bunker landed with a *THWOP*

His ears rang with an "eeeeeeeee"
While his eyes did adjust.

What could be seen,
Would be rubbish to you and me.
But to Bunker they were...

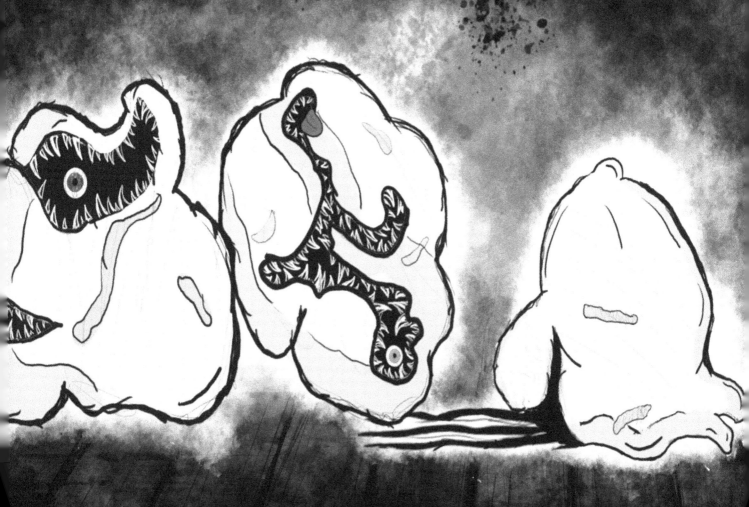

"*AWOO!*" cried Bunker,
Who cowered in fear.

Tears streamed down his jowls,
And his snot formed a bubble.

Alas, not all was lost,
For this sad loaf of bread.
The rhyme scheme returned!
And a voice filled his head.

"Be brave, even though you're small!"
His Daddy always said this.
And suddenly the darkness,
It didn't matter.
Not at all.

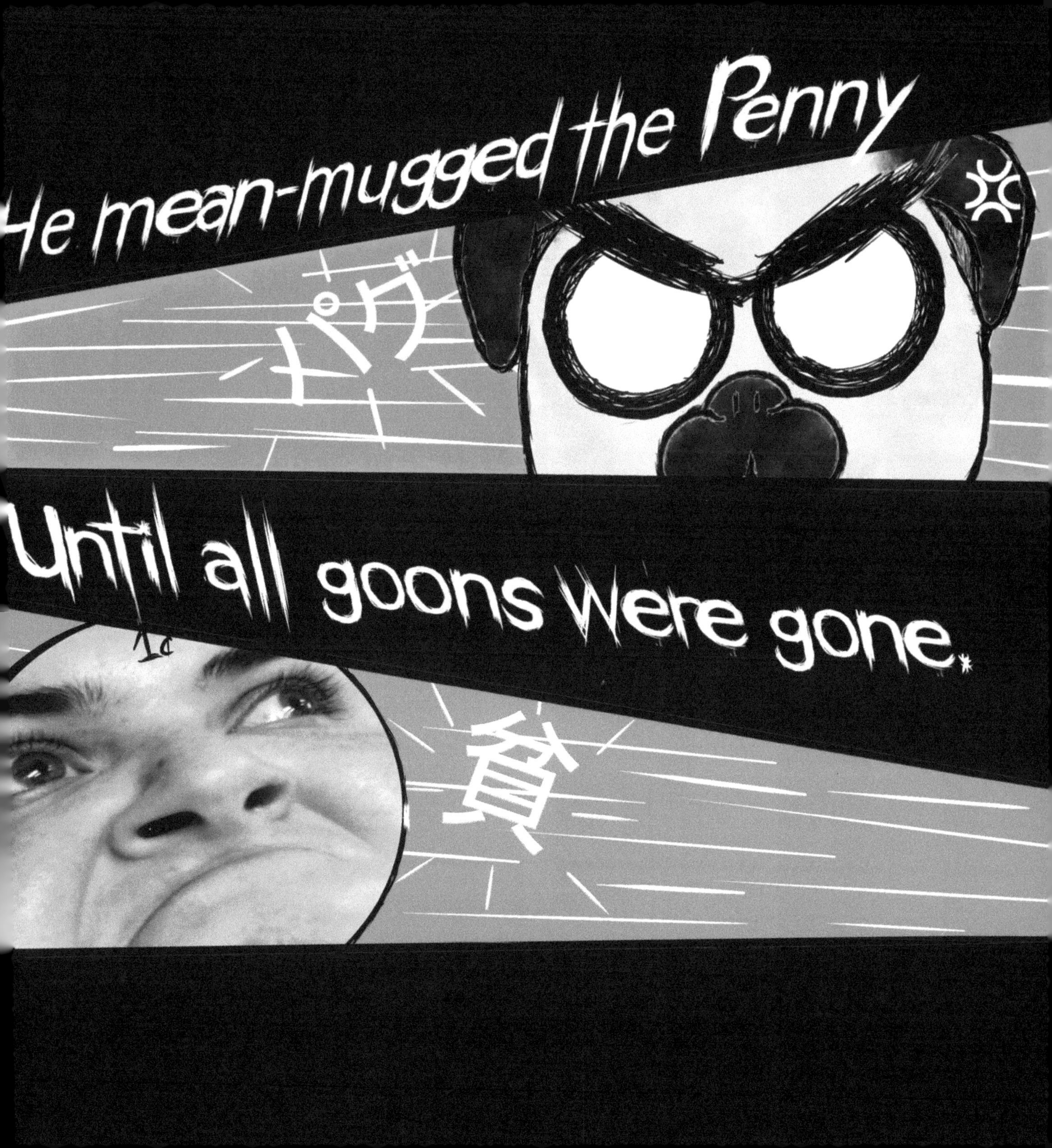
He mean-mugged the Penny
パグ
Until all goons were gone.
貧

"Ruff!" said Bunker,
For he was brave after all!
Then his eye caught a glimmer,
A way out! Down the hall!

But the darkness was not done,
It wanted him to stay.

A "Plip plop" could be heard,
Then it roared, "Puppy play!"

But before it could catch him,
He jumped through the next page!

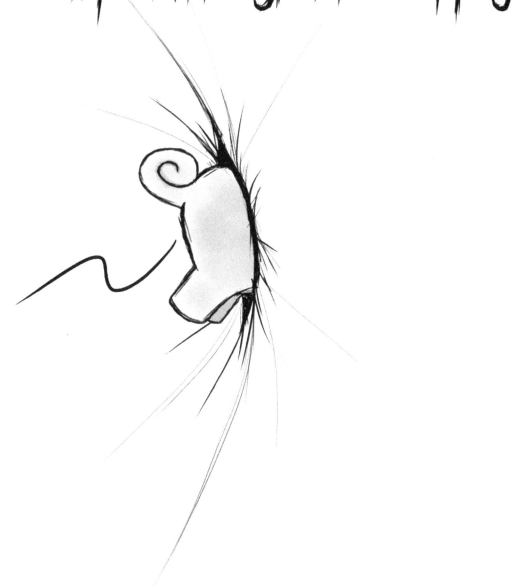

Bunker swooshed through the opening.
His eyes winced at the light.

He had beaten the terrors!
Though it took all his might.

Bunker ran from the den
And to the kitchen door.
In came his daddy,
Who got down on the floor.

He put his arms around Bunker and gave him a hug.
Thus ends our story of the brave little pug.

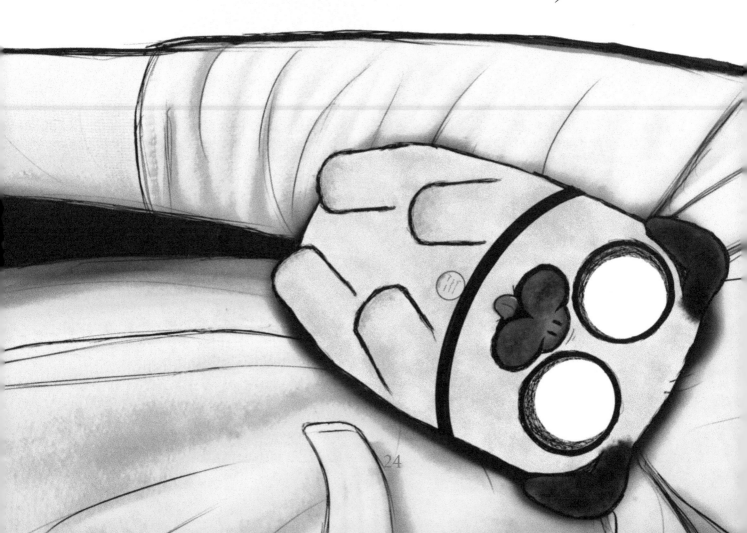

24

Or is it?

Dear Parents,

I would first like to thank you for trusting my work in your child's hands, despite how weird, dark, and gloomy it may appear. I was always drawn to books like this when I was younger, so much, in fact, that it's what inspired me to be an author. So again, thank you for being awesome.

Secondly, I was hoping to shed some personal insight that I feel everyone can benefit from. When I was a child, my mother used to take me out on the patio when it would thunderstorm. Every time the lightning struck or the thunder boomed, my mother would follow it with words of admiration. "Ooo! That was pretty!" or "Wowww! That was a loud one!" she would say. Her reasoning for doing this was due to her mother's fear of storms. My mother wanted me to see the beauty of the dark rather than to fear it. This, of course, led to me watching *Twister* on repeat until the cassette tape wore out and began my lifelong infatuation with thunderstorms.

What I'm asking is this: consider teaching your kiddos that it's okay to be afraid, but also show them the beauty in everything.

Sincerely, Austin Allyn

Published by Orange Hat Publishing 2021
ISBN 9781645382683

www.orangehatpublishing.com

To John Dilworth, Edmund McMillen, Florian Himsl, Robert Stine, Tim Burton, and Mike Thaler. This book is my love letter to all of you. I would not be the man nor the artist that I am without your inspiration into the peculiar. Thank you.

CPSIA information can be obtained
at www.ICGtesting.com
Printed in the USA
LVHW070559070721
692029LV00002B/4

9 781645 382683